# PRAISE FOR JAMIESON WOLF

"Jamieson Wolf is a gifted writer!"

**Kelley Armstrong –** New York Times Best Selling Author of the Women of the Otherworld Series

"A unique premise executed with humor, suspense and a touch of the macabre. You'll enjoy the surprising blend that Wolf brings to the world of soap operas."

**Caridad Pineiro**, *New York Times Best Selling Author of The Calling Series and Sins of the Flesh*

"Jamieson Wolf writes like Augusten Burroughs without the cynicism."

**Nasim Marie Jafry –** Author of *The State of Me*

"As I read, Jamieson Wolf taught me to dance to the beats of his heart. Heartbreaking, tender, beautiful."

**Caroline Smailes** – Author of *In Search of Adam*, *Disraeli Avenue* and *Black Boxes* and *Like Bees to Honey*

# When Love Blooms

## ~ fairy tales ~

Jamieson Wolf

**When Love Blooms**
**ISBN:** 978-0-9917580-2-9

Text: Copyright© 2015 Jamieson Wolf
Cover: Copyright© 2015 Jamieson Wolf

**Wolf Flow Press**
www.wolfflowpress.com

For Michael and

everyone who has

ever Loved and

will Love again…

# Table of Contents

~

# When Love Blooms

# The Maiden's Secret

Once upon a time, there was young maiden. She was very astute young maiden who had lots of things to say about everyone that lived in the small village of Inglewood Hamlet, which was nestled inside the walls of a great kingdom.

Every day on her way to market, she would run into Mafalda Hopplekirk, who was sleeping with the baker while already wed to the candle stick maker. Ickabod Ingleberry was sleeping with one of the scullery maids and even though he was betrothed to Paxton Plumwood, who was the daughter of the richest family in town.

Everyone had secrets, the Maiden thought. However, it took a special person to keep these secrets. She knew a lot about the people in her small hamlet, but she thought of herself as a keeper of secrets.

She would gather her knowledge of other people as if she was collecting trinkets or stamps. Secrets held power. She knew this more than anyone else in the village, for she had the most difficult secret of all.

Every morning, before the sun would rise above the stone walls of the kingdom's barriers, she would wander out of her small cottage and go to the water's edge that ran along her property line. Every house and cottage was close to a body of water; water brought life.

The Maiden knew this better than anyone. Each morning she would slip off her shift and slid slowly into the water. Once inside the waters depth's, she would only have to wait for a moment before the change began. It was no different today as she slipped into the water, letting its coldness wake her.

It always pained her when the change came; no matter how many times her body transformed itself. Closing her eyes she tried to will the pain away as her legs began to fuse together, as scales began to grow on her skin.

Soon, the water was filled with sparkling light, the magic that changed her creating a physical manifestation. Though her change filled her body with pain, it never failed to fill her with awe. - it was beautiful as well.

When the pain left her, she looked down into the water. The light of her magic was gone now. The only evidence that remained was the long tail of a fish, its scales winking at her from underneath the water.

She layed on her back in the water and let her tail splash about. She always felt more whole when she was her true self. She did not mind walking on two legs like the rest of the mortals, but always felt freer in the water.

Closing her eyes, the Maiden made a deep dive and came back up, the water splashing like diamonds around her. When she opened her eyes, she spotted a man looking at her, standing on the water's edge.

The Maiden experienced a moment of panic. She had been so busy keeping everyone else's secret that she hadn't done enough to protect her own. She stared at the man with eyes that were wide with fear. She knew that he recognized her, that he knew who she was.

"It's you." He said.

She recognized him too; he was the blacksmith's son and his name was James Ingleton. She knew that he had a kind heart and a bright spirit.

The Maiden watched with growing panic as James began to undress. Once he was completely unclothed, he walked into the water towards her. "No," she said. "Stay back please." She swam a little further out into the water. "Please stay away."

"I know what you are." James said.

The Maiden's eyes widened when lights began to bubble under the water where his feet were. As he made his way further into the water, the light around him intensified. When he was finally in front of her, the light faded. She looked down at the curving, graceful tail topped with fluttering fins.

"You're like me," the Maiden whispered. Her heart beat loudly in her chest and she wondered whether its vibrations could be felt by all of the other creatures that lived in the water.

"I am."

"I thought I was the only one." She looked into his deep greenish blue eyes and found herself looking into the sea. Instead of being turbulent, the sea that moved inside of him was calm and serene.

"So did I," he said, "Until I saw you change."

"I'm sorry," she said. "I'm hideous."

"That's not true," James replied. He moved closer to her and wrapped his arms around her waist. "I think that every part of you is beautiful." He kissed her softly on her lips and the Maiden experienced a rush of heat that ran along her skin.

"I've been waiting my whole life for you," he said.

When he kissed her again, she gave in this time, letting the pleasure run through her body. As they kissed, neither of them was aware of the light that began to bloom around them underneath the water.

They were both completely unaware of the transformation that was coming over their bodies, as their fish tails and scales faded away, leaving only mortal legs.

Instead, the Maiden had a random thought. 'Let other people keep their secrets,' she thought. 'I will take love over secrets any day.'

Still wrapped in James' embrace, the Maiden gave in completely to the power of love and let go of all of the secrets that she had held.

Taking a deep breath, she released them into the water - like a dream where they would flow away from her into the great beyond.

So the story goes...

# Revelations of a Dark Prince

Once upon a time, there was a Prince who had not known the warmth of love for some time. He was the son of the ruling family in the small kingdom that overlooked Inglewood Hamlet and its surrounding townships.

Those who worked in the castle whispered about the Prince. Some said that he worked dark magic within the stone walls of his chambers; light could be seen coming from his room at odd hours of the day and others had reported sounds of pain from inside the chamber.

When the King and Queen tried to determine what was bothering the Prince, they were met with resistance. "We only want the best for you," The King said.

"You only want an heir," The Prince would reply. "You don't want what is best for me."

"You're right," The Queen would agree. "We want what is best for the Kingdom."

It was an old argument, one that happened on a regular basis. The Prince knew that his parents loved him, that was never in question. What bothered him most was having to adhere to someone else's wishes and demands.

The truth was that the Prince was most sullen because of a secret that he carried inside him. No one could know - it was simply the way that it had to be. His kingdom needed an heir and he could not provide one if he gave into his impulses.

He had carried a flame for one of the stable boys for some time, but could never act on these feelings. The stable boy was the epitome of beauty, at least to him, but the Prince knew that he could never have him; indeed, he could never have any man.

It was the way it needed to be.

In order to assuage his growing depression about his current situation, the Prince would take to the thing he enjoyed most - wandering the forest that covered the southern half of the kingdom. There, he could wander through the trees in his true form, revelling in the freedom that it brought to him.

The moon was low on the horizon as he made his way towards the shadowy trees. The Prince did not mind the dark, for even in his mortal body he could see well in the darkness and the half light.

The pine needles crunched under his feet as he walked into the trees, letting the shadows claim him. Rather than being frightened of the darkness, the Prince found comfort instead; in the darkness, he could hide from others who expected things of him, he could hide from himself.

Cocking his head to the right, the Prince listened to the air around him. Hearing no noises that would indicate that anyone was near by, the Prince undressed, closed his eyes, and let the magic that he carried inside of him sluice over his body.

The lights that the townspeople and others in the kingdom attributed to dark magic with the devil were simply a by-product of what he was. The light filled the small glade of trees he stood in, lighting up the night with a magic that twinkled like fireflies.

When the change was done, he was on four legs. The only thing mortal that he kept in his form of a Wolf were his eyes. They looked out into the night and saw the world in shades of grey and white. The world looked simpler when it was devoid of colour and it matched the Prince's mood.

On soft feet, he padded further into the forest. He was about to put his nose low to the ground and start a hunt for some prey when he heard a noise behind him. He whipped his head around and felt his heart stop in his chest.

He was looking at the stable boy. In the half light of the coming darkness, he was truly a vision. His dark hair framed his face, and his brilliant green eyes flashed in the dusk like jewels or stars. Despite his lust addled brain, the Prince remembered that the stable boy's name was Jaxton.

Jaxton regarded the Prince in his Wolf form for some time. Then he slowly began to approach the Prince. "I won't hurt you," he said.

Not trusting himself to move, the Prince stood still. When the stable boy bent low and ran his fingers through the Prince's fur, the Prince trembled with need. No one had touched him this intimately for some time.

"That's a good boy," Jaxton said. "I've seen you around the forest before."

The Prince started. He thought that he had been careful, that he had kept his secret. He changed in the castle only when he could no longer deny his body, but the Prince had thought that he was free to do as he wished in the forest. Apparently he was mistaken.

"I keep coming here, hoping to meet someone," Jaxton said.

The Prince's heart fell slightly at these words. Of course, he thought. Someone like Jaxton would already have someone in his life. Besides, it could never amount to anything anyways. He could never be with the man he loved.

"I keep hoping to see him," Jaxton said. "It's known that he likes to come to the forest. Some say that he does dark deals in magic, but I don't believe that of him."

The Prince's heart rose. How many people were rumoured to work with dark magic in the kingdom and walked in the forest? Was the stable boy talking about him? The Prince's heart began to beat a rapid tattoo inside of his chest.

"You have his eyes." Jaxton said. "I could look into his eyes forever." The stable boy sat down next to the Prince and kept running his hands through the Prince's fur. "If I can't kiss him, at least I can kiss you."

Leaning forward, Jaxton kissed the Prince softly between his ears, planting a kiss in the soft fur that covered him. This close to him, Jaxton smelled like hay and dirt, and even the earth itself. The Prince had never smelled anything so wonderful.

When Jaxton pulled back, the Prince was startled to see a panicked look on his face. "What magic is this?" Jaxton whispered. "What are you?"

It was then that the Prince realized that the light had returned. He experienced a moment of panic; he was the only one who could control the changes, unless he waited too long or ignored the moon's pull. But he had never changed outside of his own will. What was happening to him?

The light intensified and the glade was filled with magic so bright that it was almost blinding. Jaxton had to shield his eyes, as the light was emanating from the Wolf in front of him. The townspeople would tell stories of fairies and sprites, but only the two men in the clearing knew what happened that day.

Others spread rumours of foul play, spurned on by the Prince's disappearance, but there was nothing foul about the magic in that clearing.

When the light cleared, the Prince lay naked in front of Jaxton. Jaxton's eyes took everything in - the Prince's naked form and the sight of his body. A slow smile spread along Jaxton's mouth and the Prince wondered if he had ever seen anything so beautiful.

Saying nothing, Jaxton leaned forward and kissed the Prince softly on the lips. The kiss was everything that the Prince had dreamed of. Slowly he broke away, despite his body's craving for more. "You're not afraid of me," the Prince said.

Jaxton smiled at him. "Why would I be afraid of what my heart knows?"

The Prince gave Jaxton a wry look. Jaxton laughed, the sound like water over a rock bed, and stood. "Like recognizes like," Jaxton said.

When the light began to move along Jaxton's skin, the Prince experience a moment of absolute shock. As the light cleared, another Wolf was standing in front of him. Whereas the Prince's Wolf form was graced with completely black fur, Jaxton's Wolf form was gold like the sun.

When the light faded, it left behind Jaxton, standing naked in front of him, his shredded clothes littering the ground around them. When Jaxton held out a hand to him, the Prince took it and let Jaxton help him up.

"You don't have to be alone any longer," Jaxton said.

"It is my duty to be alone," the Prince said. "I can never have you."

Jaxton raised an eyebrow and pointed to the Prince's chest. "What do you want? What does your heart want?"

The Prince didn't even need to think of the answer. "My heart wants you."

"Then your decision should be easy," Jaxton said.

He stepped away from the Prince and let the light move over his skin once more. When the light cleared, the golden Wolf stood in front of him. It walked towards the freedom the trees promised and looked back at the Prince. The Wolf barked once and its muzzle seemed to grin at him.

The decision was effortless. Letting his change come upon him, the Prince regarded the golden Wolf with need and want. When the golden Wolf went further into the trees, the Prince followed him and his heart into the shadows.

So the story goes…

# The Queen's Regret

Once upon a time, in the Kingdom that surrounded Inglewood Hamlet, there lived an unhappy Queen. She was beloved by all that knew her and the people held her in incredibly high esteem.

She had everything she could ever want or dream of having. Her wardrobes were filled with dresses in the finest silks and brocades. Her table tops were littered with perfumed water, trinkets and jewels that shone brightly when the sun slanted into her chambers.

The Queen had a loving son and a loving husband. She was the partial ruler of a prosperous land that had thrived and grown under her rule. She had everything that any one person could want, but she was miserable.

She had seen her son enter into the forest that fateful night. She did not know where he had gone, yet knew in her heart that he was still alive. She also knew that her son had had his reasons for disappearing. She hoped that he had found what he was looking for.

Her son was not the only person who walked in the forest that protected the south wall of their kingdom. Her husband did not know of her walks, or what she did there. She had to keep it that way or she would lose everything that she had.

She waited until mid day to dress. No one would think it odd that the Queen chose to walk the grounds of her kingdom, as she was almost always among the people. They loved her whole heartedly and knew that the Queen had a fondness for the trees that grew along the land.

What they did not know was that she really only had a fondness for one tree in particular. She followed the path she knew so well into the very centre of the forest. There, she came upon the small circle of trees that she recognized instantly.

The circle of birch trees never failed to take her breath away. Sunlight filtered through the thick canopy of leaves overhead, giving everything a light greenish hue. Even the air around her seemed to sparkle like emeralds.

Though all the trees in the circle were lovely, she had eyes only for one. It stood taller than the rest, in the centre of the circle. Its branches curved upwards towards the sky as if the tree had been frozen in the graceful moves of dance.

As the Queen made her way towards the tree in the centre of the circle, the tree's limbs began to shiver as if moved by a stiff breeze. There was no wind however; indeed, the Queen's hair and gown were stock still in the morning quiet.

The Queen stopped in front of the tree, leaving a few feet between herself and its roots. This was, after all, the respect that you showed to another Queen. A soft glow began to emanate from the tips of the trees branches.

When it had made its way to the tips of the ends of the roots, its glow pulsing softly like the amber hue of a million fireflies along the trees bark, the Queen had to shield her eyes. The magic that she possessed had always frightened the Queen, awing her to the point of crying.

The Dryad regarded her with an icy glare. "Why are you here Mafalda?"

The Queen regarded the Dryad with a guarded stare. "I wanted to see you, Tiana." The name hurt the Queen's lips, as if a sharp barb was lodged there, prickling at her tongue. "I think my son has gone in search of love." The Queen put a hand to her heart. "It made me remember our times, the ones we shared."

The Dryad's glare hardened. "You dare." The words were a hiss, a sharp crackle of leaves that moved and shook the branches of the trees in the circle. Though there was no wind, the Queen heard the sharp rattle of wind passing through tree limbs.

"You dare speak of that." The Dryad came closer, the roots of her tree reaching out and around her to form a chair that was like a throne. She sat, almost gracefully, regarding the Queen with a frigid stare. "This is all that remains of my people." She gestured with a hand that was etched with lines that were like vines.

The Queen knew that the Dryad's entire body had those marks. The tattoos covered her skin in green ink that pulsed and moved with a power all of its own. Tiana's body was covered with the markings of her people: leaves, vines, lines of bark etched into her skin like grooves along her back.

"I am sorry," the Queen said. She knew that these words were not enough, that they did not express the pain that throbbed inside of her heart like the sharp poke of a branch, stabbing into her. "I cannot tell you how sorry."

The Dryad laughed, the sound like the caws of the crows that even now regarded the Queen from the branches of the trees that formed the circle. "You chose him over me."

Tears slid down the Queen's face. "I had to, don't you see? I had no other choice."

"You could have stayed with me." The Dryad took a deep breath, the ground beneath her shuddering with the effort. "I loved you. I gave you everything." When the Dryad released her breath, the branches of the trees shook, scattering the crows that had been perched there. They flew into the sky like a black cloud, spreading out across the expanse of bluish grey sky like an ink blot. "But you chose to save your reputation."

"Two of our kind can't be together." The Queen said. "A mortal and a Dryad?" As tears slid down the Queen's cheeks, she did nothing to stop them.

"That's not what bothered you," the Dryad said. She shook her head. "That was never what bothered you."

Standing, the Dryad regarded the Queen with a glare that snapped and crackled like broken wood. In that look, the Queen saw her only regret and the heart that she had shattered. When the Dryad went to move back into her tree, the Queen held out a hand, touching her.

"Wait," she said. The words were a whisper and the Queen could barely speak them. "Please wait."

The Dryad stopped. She did not turn, but she did not walk away. "Speak your peace."

The Queen knew that she only had mere moments to speak, that she had to make every word count. "It should have been you," she said. She whispered the words, saying for the first time what she had known all along but could never utter aloud. "It has always been you. I live with what I did to you every day of my life."

The Dryad stiffened, her branches shuttering and snapping along the ground. "Why do you speak this way?"

"Because my Prince went in search of love. I know this. I can feel his heart beating stronger. I always spoke to him of duty, but I never spoke to him of love." Taking a deep breath, the Queen said the words she had been holding in for so many years. "I don't want my life to end with you being my biggest regret."

When the Dryad turned to face the Queen, Mafalda saw what she should have seen all along. The Dryad was not looking at her with hate, but with pain - pain that the Queen had put there.

The Queen stepped forward and wrapped her arms around the Dryad, who in return clutched the Queen in her embrace. When the two kissed, flowers bloomed along the ground in the thousands, in the hundreds of thousands. There were flowers of ever shape, size and colour.

The people that lived in the small township of Inglewood Hamlet had plenty to gossip about when the Queen, their own beloved Queen, disappeared only three days after her the Prince's disappearance.

Some whispered that the Prince had taken the Queen off into the forest to show her dark magic. Some said that the Queen had met with treachery. Yet only the King really knew the truth.

One morning, as he wandered the forest in his grief seven days after his Queen's disappearance, he had come upon a small circle of trees, a glade that was filled with light and the sound of birdsong. The ground was covered with thousands of flowers of every colour.

Standing in the centre of the circle was a tree of such beauty; it nearly stopped the Kings heart. Wrapped around the tree, as if in a soft caress, was a scattering of ivy. It flowed along the trunk of the tree and traced itself along some of the trees branches, as if the two were entwined in an embrace.

Lying on the ground in front of the tree was the Queen's crown.

So the story goes…

# Murder of a Crow's Heart

Once upon a time, in the badlands that surrounded the eastern side of the Kingdom near Inglewood Hamlet, a crow circled the skies.

Some in the small village of Inglewood Hamlet said that the crow was actually three, able to reform and take shape at will. Some said that the bird was made of smoke and thunder, and would grant wishes if you were lucky enough to capture it in your net.

The carrion bird knew of the opinions of the townspeople, but what the small minded people of Inglewood Hamlet didn't realize was that the crow was actually a Crow. He had a job to do it didn't matter whether he wanted to do it or not
After all, he thought, needs must. He knew this better than anyone.

As he swooped down from the dark skies that hid him almost completely, he let his wings stretch out to his sides. Soon, he heard the flutter of fabric in the air as his body reformed, clothed in the long dark robes that symbolized his station in life.

He sighed in contentment when his feet graced the red sand. He didn't mind flying, but he preferred his human form. Though he could change forms like the wind, every time he lost a feather a part of him went floating away on the wind.

Sometimes, when he shifted back, he would be missing a lock of hair or perhaps an eyebrow. Tired of losing hair, the Crow had shaved off all of his body hair, only to discover the next time when he lost a feather, he also lost pieces of his skin.

From then on, he made sure to grow his hair long, well past his shoulders. It ended in lustrous curls at the small of his back and framed his angular face like two slashes of midnight.

His robes moved in the still, humid air that surrounded him. As he walked, the robe flittered and moved around him as if moved by a soft breeze. His hair did the same, almost crackling with the magic that ran inside of him.

Following the pull that resonated inside of his stomach like a glowing ember, the Crow went towards his charge. He had been helping people cross over for centuries. It hurt every time. Each time, the dead were required to pay a price for their travels. He may bring them to the other side of the curtain, but a piece of them remained in him.

Of all of those that he carried inside of him, there was one that was the sweetest. Against his better nature the Crow had saved him, only to lose his heart to him instead. The townsfolk called him and his Brothers a Murderer of Crows as they all wore the dark wings of the black bird when they shifted form. It seemed an appropriate description for what had been done to his heart.

The Crow wondered why, after all these years, he would spare a thought for the mortal man-child. He should have known by now, however, that there is no such thing as a coincidence. The Fates, sitting somewhere in the stars, were probably laughing at him.

As he walked towards the pull that indicated someone who had passed on, he was surprised when the pulse of the pull changed. As he moved closer to his target, the flame of light inside of him became a beacon.

There was only one person, one mortal, who had evoked such a reaction from him. He was not surprised to find Bastien standing in front of him. He had been waiting at the edge of the badlands, coming as close as any mortal could.

When Bastien saw the Crow he stood, his eyes filled with something that the Crow remembered was called hope. He came to a stop mere inches from the man he loved more than words and did not touch him. "Why are you here?"

"I didn't think you'd come." Bastien smiled and the Crow's heart broke a little more.

"That's not what I asked you." The Crow knew that his rough voice, the darkness of it mixed with the rasp of a crow's beak, was far from the warmth that Bastien wanted.

"Mikhail?" Bastien's voice was filled with need. "Mikhail, what's wrong? Aren't you happy to see me?" He tried to come closer, but was stopped by the barrier. Any mortal who set foot in the badlands without some kind of magic would perish. Bastien, as a mere mortal, had no such magic.

"Why are you here?" He asked again.

"I was trying to find you," Bastien said. He reached out to him, but the Crow moved away. "You left me, without a word." There was pain in Bastien's voice. "That night that I saw you in the clearing in the forest."

"I still wish that you had never seen me," the Crow said.

"Why, Mikhail?"

"I am death," he said. "I am a monster." The Crow turned away from Bastien and began to walk away. "There is no way that two people from two different races can be together." He hung his head and his robes fluttered around him with a soft, whispery sigh. "It is the way it must be."

The Crow had taken only a few steps when Bastien spoke behind him. "Who says it must be this way?"

He turned with a whisper, his robes fluttering out behind him with the wind that he had created. "It has always been this way, it is the right way."

"But how can it be the right way if we're not together?" Bastien asked.

"You saw me take a life. I had wished for you to never see me that way, never to see me for what I am." He turned his head away; it hurt to look at Bastien, hurt to still crave his touch. "I am a monster."

Bastien shook his head. "I saw you help someone in pain find comfort. It was the most beautiful thing that I have ever seen." He paused here, swallowing, as if trying to find the words. "You are the most beautiful thing that I have ever seen."

Here, Bastien reached out as if he would be able to touch him. "You are the most beautiful thing that I have ever seen."

Tears slid down the Crow's face. "You can't mean that."

"But I do," Bastien said. "I love all of you, even the parts of yourself that you don't love."

"Even if such a thing were possible, how could we be together? I am death."

"Would you leave it behind if it meant having me for as long as you wanted me?"

The Crow didn't even have to think about his answer. "Yes."

"Then the choice has already been made," Bastien said. He held out his hand again to the Crow and Mikhail took it. When he stepped from the badlands to the grass, a sharp pain ran down his body, as if something inside wanted to get out.

Light began to stream around him as an unseen breeze lifted Mikhail into the air. His hair and robes whipped around him as the wind grew in density and power. Bastien covered his eyes as the wind riled around Mikhail in a gale force.

When there was silence once again, Bastien opened his eyes. What he saw filled him with hope. Mikhail lay on the grass in front of him, wearing a simple tunic and soft, black breeches that shone in the half light of dusk.

It was the missing hair that gave Bastien hope. Instead of his long locks that fell in ringlets past his shoulders, his head was shaven. White stubble glittered along his palate like a scattering of stars.

Mikhail took Bastien's arm and stood gently. A wind blew around them softly, as if pushing pulling them more closely together. Mikhail put a hand up and felt the stubble that used to be his hair, his feathers. More tears welled in his eyes, but this time they were tears of joy. "They have taken their price," he said.

"What does that mean?" Bastien whispered.

"It means that I am no longer immortal." Mikhail moved closer and took the man he loved into his arms. Mikhail kissed Bastien softly on the lips, tasting him.

"I am no longer immortal, but I am yours for all eternity," he said.

Kissing the man he loved more than anything, Mikhail gave into the passion that he had denied himself and began to believe in the joy of possibilities.

So the story goes…

# The King's Lament

Once upon a time, in the kingdom that surrounded the small township of Inglewood Hamlet, there lived an unhappy King. He was often in dark moods, and the townspeople of Inglewood Hamlet regularly wondered about the state of their King.

After all, they said, he had lost a lot in a short time. A stable boy had wandered off never to be seen again and one of the cooks was missing. That did not cover the grief the King was suffering due to the missing Queen and Prince.

The search had begun when the Prince had not returned after thirteen hours. When the Queen had gone missing three days later, the search was intensified. Bloodhounds searched the land for the missing members of the royal family.

As the weeks went forward and summer moved into fall, the King could be seen wandering the edge of the forest where both his wife and son had last been seen. It was now said that the forest, indeed that the whole Kingdom, was cursed. The townspeople of Inglewood Hamlet had many varying opinions on the nature of this curse, but one thing was for certain: these were dark days indeed.

Only the King really knew where both the Prince and Queen had gone. He had left the Queen's crown at the base of the tree covered with vines. It seemed only right. He knew that his wife was not dead. He knew that she lived on, that she had chosen a different form in order to be with another.

The same was true of his son. He had claimed the form that his magic had gifted him in order to love another. Some would wonder if his wife and son had changed themselves in order to have what they needed. But the towns' people never really knew the truth, they could only speculate and gossip.

The King, who was wise and kind, knew that this was not so. He knew that the Queen and Prince had let go and claimed their true selves. He was not bitter that his wife had gone back to the woman she had always loved. He knew that the Dryad held his wife's heart, just as he knew that the stable boy held his son's.

Though he said little, the King saw all. Some thought him sharp tongued, others thought him moody and quiet. All found him just and fair, however. Part of this had to do with his ability to speak only when it was absolutely necessary.

It was a learned habit. It kept his family away from him, but it made him a fair ruler. He now realized that it also made him a lonely one. He would often wonder the forest alone, hoping to regain his sense of tranquility.

He knew that beauty existed in the world, but he had never been able to see it. He had always been too busy ruling over a land that he loved and ignored those around him that he was supposed to love. There was beauty in the world, but not for someone like him.

Passing by the circle of trees where his wife's form was stretched like a caress over the limbs of the tree of the Dryad, he experienced a moment of pain that flared inside of him like a tongue of fire. He hadn't felt this sensation in some time, but he still recognized it- it was desire.

Desire for what, the King did not know. He had many regrets in his life and he often wondered and thought long about how to right his past so that he could enjoy his present. But he was never able to find a satisfactory answer.

He wandered further away from the grove of trees and made his way further into the forest. He moved past a small rock face whose surface was covered with a scattering of mica that shimmered like water in the early morning light. As he moved past a large slice of tall grass, the King heard singing.

When the King saw who possessed the voice that thrilled him and evoked emotions inside of him at the same time. It was his Fool, Skulton. He sang in a clear, bright tenor that lit a flame inside of the King, one that had lain dormant for some time.

It was not the voice that stopped the King in his tracks however, though Skulton's voice was incredibly beautiful. It was the fact that he was glowing. Even as he sang, the glow that emanated from Skulton's skin intensified until the clearing was filled with light that was as bright as the daytime.

The King had carried a flame for the Fool inside of himself for some time; if he was honest with himself, he loved Skulton. The Fool was the only person who understood him, who knew him as he truly was. The same could not be said for Skulton. The King had no inclination that his Fool might be an immortal.

Yet the evidence was right in front of him. He was a sensible man, but he believed in the unknown; hadn't his wife become part of a tree and his son a Wolf? His decision made, the King stepped further into the clearing, the forest alive around him. The Fool sensed the King's movement and the singing stopped almost at once. "You didn't have to stop," the King said. "That was beautiful."

Bowing his head, the Fool averted his eyes. "I never meant for you to see me like this."

"But you're beautiful," the King said. "I have never seen such beauty."

When Skulton looked at him, the King saw what had always been there but he had always been to busy pushing people away from him to notice it. There was love in his Fool's eyes, love that bloomed like sunshine, blinding him.

"I'm glad you think it's beautiful," the Fool said. "I was singing about you."

The flame that had been light flared brightly. "About me?"

"You are so selfless and honourable. You rule a Kingdom but think nothing of your own joy or your own heart. Mine aches for you."

Despite himself, the King moved closer to Skulton, taking in his tall, broad shouldered frame, the rough tangle of dark hair that framed his face, bells attached to the ends of his hair with string.

"Why would your heart ache for me?" These words came out in a harsh whisper that lent heat to the King's words. That heat was filled with need.

"Because you do not know love."

The King shrugged; had he been a bird, he would have ruffled his feathers. "What is love?" the King replied.

"Let me show you," Skulton said.

Moving with a grace that no mortal man was blessed with, Skulton took the King in his arms and kissed him. When Skulton's lips met the King's, the King experienced such a rush of emotion that it was as if a flock of candles had been lit inside of him, their flames dancing like wings.

Heat rushed along his skin and he found himself kissing Skulton back, trying to put everything he had ever felt about Skulton into the kiss. His Fool seemed to understand the King's need as he changed the angle of the kiss and took it deeper.

The King broke the kiss, needing to take air into his lungs to steady his swimming senses. When he looked up at Skulton, he saw love there, such pure and whole love that his body quaked with need for it. The King touched his Fool's face with calloused fingers, running them down Skulton's jaw and chin.

"You know," the King said, "For a Fool, you are pretty wise."

Skulton kissed the King softly on his lips. "I get that a lot," he said. "But everyone needs to be foolish every once in a while. It is not a life fully lived if all you think about is others and not yourself."

"But that's all I know how to do," the King said. "I have never learned to truly love another person."

"Then let me show you," Skulton said. "We can learn together."

When his Fool touched his lips to the King's once more, the King wrapped his arms around Skulton and gave into the love blooming inside of him.

So the story goes…

# Sad Songs for a Scullery Maid

Once upon a time, there was a woman who did not love herself. Sheenagh Lonelyheart had seen a lot of good people come and go. She had seen a lot of bad people come and go, too, for that matter. Not much in life fazed her anymore. The people of Inglewood Hamlet were a disgusting bunch and she would be happy if the whole lot of them died in a freak storm that wiped out half the county; but left her ale house alone, thank you very much, she thought.

Some of the people in Inglewood Hamlet thought they were well to do, because a great bloody castle sat above them like a chess piece, its shadow seeming to stretch along the whole of Inglewood.

The Kingdom of Inglewood resided on the countryside of the Inglewood Township, which was home to Inglewood Hamlet. Sheenagh sighed. The town planners had sure dropped the bull's testicles on that one.

When Thom Fowlery began to tinker the ivory keys of her harpsichord, she cringed. He tinkled out a happy tune that set her teeth on edge and quickly got on her last nerve. Sheenagh knew that she should encourage the happy banter within her establishment, but she was in no mood for that today.

Scullery maids, and other people in her caste system, were dependent upon the good will of others. Sheenagh's problem was that she hated most people. She did see the irony in owning an ale house where people would come to gather while she disliked other people with a passion bordering on absolute hate. She didn't like the people that frequented her establishment; she liked their money instead.

Wiping a glass with a clean rag, Sheenagh recalled her mother's words. "Why would you want to run an ale house? You can't stand most people, you can't even stand yourself! Why would you take part in such foolishness?"

Sheenagh had no answer then, and she had no answer now. The truth was that she had dreamed of running her own establishment since she had been a girl child of only seven summers. Even then, she knew that it was probably the wrong kind of profession for her. She had been a prickly child, quick to anger. As she had gotten older, her temper had proceeded her, giving her a reputation of a woman of ill repute.

She couldn't give two farting flying crows what other people thought of her. As she always told herself, other people's opinions were none of her business. That famous temper flared to life as Thom Fowlery began tinkering away, little notes ringing out into the air, pulsing with happiness that had long been denied to Sheenagh. With an angry slash of her arms, she motioned to Thom. "Stop that, stop that this instant."

Thom stopped playing (he followed directions well, something most men could not claim) and looked up at her. "What is it Sheenagh?" He asked. "Is something wrong?"

Sheenagh's temper flared when he grinned at her, the corners of his mouth rising up in a half smile. She wanted to spit in his face. "Yeah, there is. We're closed."

"But you've still got a few more hours of business," Thom said.

"Don't tell me how to run my own show, Thom Fowlery. Otherwise, I might be tempted to tell your kind goodwife what you've been doing with your stable boy. I think she might be very interested to know who you've really been playing hide the purple flower with, instead of the maid likes she thinks, eh Thom?"

Thom nodded and stood. Most of the patrons had heard the exchange and filed out of the doors. She closed it gladly behind the last customer and took a deep breath. The ale house was filled with silence, gorgeous silence, and she revelled in it momentarily.

Her momentary iota of peace was interrupted by the sound of bells; they filled the air around her with a sound of such clear beauty. Despite her ever constant bad mood, Sheenagh experienced a moment of lightness that could have been considered true emotion.

She hadn't felt such an emotion since the passing of dear Goodman Brown, who had been the love of her life - the only love of her life as it turned out. Turning towards the sound, Sheenagh wiped tears from her face, the first that she had cried since the passing of her husband.

Sitting at the harpsichord was the most beautiful man Sheenagh had ever seen. He was tall, she could tell that even though he was sitting down. He had long blond hair that flowed well past his shoulders. It glowed in the half light of her ale house. But that wasn't the only thing glowing.

She may have helped herself to a few pints of barley ale, but Sheenagh was almost positive that he was glowing too, that thin whips of light were emanating from his skin. The song had been beautiful, but this man was more beautiful still.

Sheenagh wiped at the tears that were sliding down her cheeks absentmindedly. "What are you?" she asked.

"What makes you think that I'm any more than a man?" he asked.

"No man plays like that." Sheenagh said. "I haven't felt such emotion since…" She tried to clear her head, to see past the wall of feelings that had risen inside of her. "I have never felt such emotions," she said simply.

"That is because you've never allowed yourself to feel them. But sometimes it takes a moment of true beauty to help you see more clearly."

Sheenagh looked more closely at him. "What do they call you Sir?"

The man stood from the harpsichord and bowed to her. "I am Paeder., he said.

"And what of your lineage?"

"I have none," he said. "It is not necessary."

"But lineage is always necessary!" Sheenagh said shrilly. "How else can we know where we came from?"

"We only need to grasp where we came from to get where we are going," he said. "Where there is beauty, there are possibilities." He walked towards her. "You just have to be open to it."

"What are you?" Sheenagh had come to the conclusion that Paeder was not mortal; no one could sparkle like he did or play the keys like he did if he were a mere mortal. She knew that there were other beings that lived amongst them in Inglewood Hamlet. Sheenagh had just never come face to face with one of them.

"Are you sure you want to hear the answer?" Paeder asked.

"Of course I do!" Sheenagh said. "Otherwise, why would I have asked?"

"Mortals are always asking things that they think they want to know the answer to, but they don't really want to hear the truthful answer. It seems to be a great paradox of your kind." He smiled at her kindly.

"What are you?" She asked again. The words came out in a whisper.

The glow that covered him increased, brightening the room. "I'm an angel," he said simply, giving her another bow. "At your service, Sheenagh Lonleyheart."

"Angels?" Sheenagh regarded the Goodman Paeder with something that was close to disdain. "You don't expect me to believe in wive's tales, do you?"

Paeder smiled at her. "Angels are actually more common than you think they are." He walked closer towards her. As he did so, Sheenagh noticed his shadow.

It stretched along the wooden planks and tables of her ale house, reminding her of the castle of Inglewood when the sun was at its zenith at the height of midday; it would move along the town streets until its shadow covered all of them.

The children would wait by the bakery steps, hoping to be lucky enough to be one of the chosen who would be standing near the turrets that topped the castles tower. They would play amongst the shadow turrets playing war games or they would re-enact fairy tales.

But that shadow always looked like a castle, no matter how far it stretched. The Goodman Paeder's was different. His shadow showed his legs. his arms and his head. On either side of him, where she could see nothing but air, his shadow showed a great span of wings.

As he made his way towards her and closer to the door, the shadow wings moved with him, their feathers seeming to touch everything. Though she could not feel any feathers as he brushed by her, she did indeed hear their rustle, their soft whisper as they moved along her skin.

He turned to face her. "Will you think on what I've said, Goodwife Proudlove?"

Sheenagh shook her head. "My name is Lonleyheart."

"I don't think so." Paeder said. "Look inside yourself, and you will know the truth." He reached out then and touched her breastbone, just above her heart that beat quickly. A warmth that had been absent for a long time began to flow through her.

"Everyone has the power to love themselves, if they let themselves do so," he said. Reaching up, Paeder touched her jaw line, the heat spreading there as well. Eyes that had only been able to see the blackness in the world could now see how beautiful the world was around her. Even the shabbiness of her ale house held a certain kind of charm.

He leaned in and kissed her softly on the lips. When Sheenagh would later tell her tale to the patrons of her ale house who inquired over her remarkable transformation, Sheenagh would say that it was as if she could no longer say a mean word about anyone. Not only that, she would say, she didn't even have any mean spirits left in her.

"It was as if the power of loving myself washed away whatever blackness remained," she would say. Those who listened, in awe of the glow that came from her skin and the brightness that sparkled in her eyes, didn't doubt her words at all. For what else but an angel could bring about such a dramatic change in the horrible Sheenagh Lonleyheart?

When he opened the door to go back out into the streets of Inglewood Hamlet, the sun was almost at its full height for the day. The light filtered in past the Goodman Paeder who was framed by the doorway.

Sheenagh saw the fullness of his wings for but an instant, but she saw them clearly. They stretched behind him, as tall and as broad as their shadows had indicated. They were of a gorgeous bluish white plumage that pulsed and shone with magic.

When Sheenagh blinked, the Goodman Paeder was gone and she stood bathed in the sun's shadow alone. For the first time that she could remember, the sun filled Sheenagh with hope - Hope that shone through.

So the story goes...

# Bells that Sing for a Blacksmith

Once upon a time in the village of Inglewood Hamlet, there lived a blacksmith by the name of Christopher Irwinian. Many in the village said that he had once been in line to be a Knight, but had given it up and chosen smithing as a profession instead.

Many in the village wondered why Irwinian would make such a choice when he could have taken on a profession that made more money, thirty gold pieces a year easy, plus a strong benefits package and a goose during Yule. Who could ask for more?

Yet instead of a life of riches, Irwinian worked on his smithing instead. He made many things that bettered the village of Inglewood Hamlet. He made the iron fastenings for all the fences, the latches for their gates, the locks for their houses.

He made wrought iron fences for the library, benches and chairs for the elderly to sit on out in the town square. He even made the chimes for the church bells that would ring and call everyone to service, their voices ringing out across the sky.

But the one thing he made more than any other object was sculptures. Poured and sculpted from moulds, the detail were so fine that they would appear real. Many speculated over who these sculptures were of, for they were all the same woman.

Many in Inglewood Hamlet speculated over who the mystery woman was. Some said that the woman was someone the blacksmith had known while he sailed at sea; some speculated that she was a woman that he had met on a distant island.

Others said that she was the lost love that he still mourned for, after he had lost her hand in a duel with an arch enemy. Some said that he was enchanted at night by a beautiful mermaid that appeared in his dreams.

No one knew the truth however. Christopher Irwinian was actually sculpting a ghost.

Day after day he saw her walking through the streets, slipping into alleyways, standing under shop awnings, their wooden signs swinging in the breeze. But he knew that she was lost to him. He wondered if he was in love with a ghost, or a spirit. Perhaps she was a guardian angel?

He believed in such beings and knew that they presented themselves from time to time. But he could not know this for sure. All that he did know was that he couldn't get her image out of his mind's eye.

So while he worked on small sets of chimes or delicately shaped pots, chains and pieces of jewellery, he also sculpted the mysterious ghost woman who haunted him. Late at night, when he was alone at home in his small suite of rooms above his smith shop, he wondered after the woman.

She had flowing dark brown hair that bounced around her shoulders in curls. Intelligent and dark eyes would stare at him for a moment before she would disappear, as if vanishing into fog.

He wondered if he was losing his mind or going insane; neither of which appealed to him. So instead, he sculpted her. Soon, he had created thirty or forty sculptures of her; they filled his rooms and his small shop.

Christopher was in the act of placing some of the sculptures in the front of his shop when a shadow fell across his smith shop doorway. The fire was hot and crackling behind him and was throwing off a lot of light, so Christopher could only see a shadowy outline.

The woman was wearing a soft dress that swept the floorboards of his shop. As she walked towards him, the wind swept into the shop, bringing a welcome breeze. It fluttered her hair and, for a moment, the woman seemed to shimmer.

Then she stepped further into his establishment and Christopher's breath left him. The shimmer did not leave her skin; instead it continued to dance along her skin, swirling in the air. It was a light that was brighter than any fire could make.

"You can see me for who I am," the woman said. It wasn't a question.

"I know that you are not like other women, Goodwife," Christopher said. He wondered if this was one of the angels that walked amongst them. The other villagers had other names for people like this: the Fey, the Fair Folk, Those from the Veil. Christopher tended instead to think of them as angels, beings of light that the world could never understand.

But he had never been approached by one before.

She must have seen the expression on his face, for she smiled and held out her hands from her sides. "Don't be afraid. I am merely saying what I already know; for how could you not see the world differently to sculpt what you do?"

Christopher wiped his brow. With the fire behind him and the woman in front of him, heat was rising inside of him. The woman emanated such a feeling of love that it was impossible for him not to blush.

"Thank you," he said. He wondered if he would even be able to say any more than that. The woman, sensing his discomfort moved forward again.

"Don't be afraid, I don't wish to harm you." She smiled and held out her hand to him. "You may call me Suzanne."

Christopher knew enough of folklore to ask, "Is that your true name?"

"I have many names," Suzanne said, "But that is the name you can call me by."

He nodded and swallowed thickly. "And what is it that I can do for you, Lady?"

"I have been watching you for many months. I like to step amongst the mortals from time to time. In this little village, it is you who interests me the most."

Christopher's heart beat more quickly. His grandmother had once told him that it would not do to attract the interest of those that walked amongst them. "It is often trouble and best avoided," she would say, "But if you do happen to cross the path of one, respect them as you do me and you'll be fine."

"Why would that be Lady?" he asked.

"As I've watched you, I've seen you fall both in and out of love just as quickly. Instead of bringing you joy, your love, or your idea of love, has brought you sorrow."

She gestured at the sculptures of the ghost, the spirit that haunted him at night and interrupted his thoughts during the daylight hours. "Love can sometimes burn bright, but it is best not to chase love that is not possible and focus instead on what is possible."

She raised an eyebrow at him. "Do you get my meaning, Goodman Irwinian?"

He was not surprised that she knew his name, but he wondered at her advice. "I don't understand you," he said.

She laid a hand along the cheek of one of his sculptures. "I see her too," she said. "I see many things that others cannot. It is best that you let her go." Her voice softened. "You are keeping her here."

Suzanne's words sent a slight chill down his spine that tempered the heat of the fire. "But I love her," he whispered.

"You cannot love what cannot be," she replied. "True love can burn bright like the most brilliant star, but like a comet that falls from the heavens, it can fade just as quickly."

She reached forward and wiped a tear from his cheek. Christopher had not been aware that he was crying. "Do not cry for what could not be. Only embrace what can."

At her touch, a calmness spread through him that comforted the recesses of his heart. His soul was more refreshed than it had ever been. "But I long for beauty, for joy," he said.

"You have beauty. Do you not sculpt the bells that ring in the bell tower of the village square?"

Christopher nodded. "That I do, Lady."

"And do they not bring you joy every time they ring? Every time they sing into the air and call those who listen towards it?"

Christopher nodded again. "They do."

She smoothed out her hand and held his face. "That is true beauty. That is the essence of beauty. When your bells sing, their song is like peals of joy that touch all of those that hear them."

She leaned forward and placed a kiss on his temple. When she withdrew, her glow intensified, the swirl of blue magic that covered her skin flickering like a candle flame. "Do not chase the love that was. Only embrace the love that is possible, the love that is within yourself."

Closing his eyes, Christopher embraced the feeling of calm that ran through him at the woman's touch. When he opened his eyes, she was standing at the door to his shop once more.

"Are you leaving so soon, Lady?"

She smiled at him. "You know where to find me and how to call for me," she said.

When he blinked the woman was gone, but he did see a blue glow that danced at the edges of the forest across the field from his smith shop, the one that surrounded one side of Inglewood Hamlet. The blue glow moved like a star through the branches of the trees and, as Christopher watched, made its way into the sky.

It settled itself in between a nest of clouds. Christopher could see the star winking in between the light that came before darkness. It burned brighter than all the rest.

As the evening passed, Christopher thought of the woman. She could only be a star, he thought, for what other explanation was there? Looking at his sculptures, their forms covered in shadow from the crackling fire, he turned back to look at the blue star that shone above the tree branches.

Taking only a moment to make his decision, Christopher stepped out of his smith shop and walked towards the forest.

That evening, the villagers of Inglewood Hamlet experienced something that could only fall into the realm of the unexplained. Some say that they saw a ghost, a pale slip of a woman, floating through the sky. Goodwife Prudence Merryweather swore she saw the ghost slip past her bedroom as she emptied her chamber pot.

Others said that they saw two blue lights, slipping in and out of the branches of the trees that made up the forest, their brightness almost blinding.

Only one thing could be agreed upon: the villagers of Inglewood Hamlet had seen something extraordinary.

No one ever saw the blacksmith again. Some in the village said that had gone in search of the woman he had sculpted so often. They had no idea how close to the truth they were.

Yet every time the bells rang, at sunup, midday and sundown, every villager experienced such a moment of joy that it was as if they were filled to the brim with it.

So the story goes...

# The Seer's Curse

Once upon a time, in the Village of Inglewood Hamlet, there lived a woman who could see everything yet wished that she could see nothing.

Prudence Merryweather has always been able to see. Even when she was a small child, she had always been able to *see* what others could not. She knew, for instance, that her mother was lying with the stable boy and that her father was lying with the mild maid that lived and worked on their holding of land. Her brother Eustace, who was her heart, was in love with a woman who could not love him back.

The Kingdom of Inglewood resided on the countryside of the Inglewood Township, which was home to Inglewood Hamlet.

On one side were the forests, thick and large like ivy dipped in thorns; on the other, her mountains. The two remaining sides were guarded by desert that stretched far and wide, canvasses of sand that reflected the light, and a terrain where nothing of beauty grew.

Had Prudence known that those deserts would become her home when she was a young girl, she would have laughed. But seeing as she saw, she could find no humour in the situation.

When she was a young girl, she had told her parents what she had seen, that she knew of their misconduct. Her father had responded by locking her in her room until she was older.

Those in the Village of Inglewood Hamlet speculated about why Goodman Merryweather would shut his daughter away in the tallest tower of their stone dwelling. Some said that she held a family secret that would ruin them if it was released out into the open.

Others in the village said Prudence possessed such breathtaking beauty that she must be shut away from prying eyes, lest she blind them with her beauty.

For Prudence, the truth was far simpler: her parents feared what they did not understand. But she didn't understand it either; she did not ask to see, did not ask to know the goings on of others.

It was only when her brother had died that she was able to leave home. For weeks, she would see a haze of red covering Eustace's face whenever she looked at him. It would drip from his mouth when he spoke, sliding like snakes over the glaze of his eyes.

Prudence begged him not to leave the house, not to go. But it didn't matter what she said nor did; she could never change what would be. Three days later, Eustace was found dead on the main road that led into the Village.

The lawmen said that he had met his end at the hands of bandits; Prudence was able to confirm it, and had even told the lawmen where to find them and how they had done it. When this information turned out to be true, Prudence's family feared her more than ever. Leaving home, she took a room in a boarding house and tried to set out on her own life.

It was not easy. For years she was alone, but saw in her heart that there was someone who waited for her, someone who would take away her pain. When she met Lord Woodthorne, Prudence thought that she had found the man who would make her heart swell with love. But love blinded her to the truth and for once she could not see what her fate would be.

He had always said that he loved all of her, that he saw into her and loved her completely. She should have known from her years of experience that this would not be the case- that he would leave her, too. But love blinds us to even the things that we know are true in our heart of hearts.

When she warned Woodthrone about the impending death of his sister, he stared at her aghast. "How do you know this?" He asked her. "Are you a Witch?"

Prudence had shaken her head. "No, far from it. I see. Your sister is in danger. I can't let you lose her as I lost my brother."

But in the end, Woodthrone had lost his sister and Prudence had lost him. When his sister's death actually transpired, Lord Woodthorne, the one man who had said he had loved her completely, could no longer look at her the same way.

And so Prudence had resolved herself to her life alone. The talk about her in the village increased and she encouraged every rumour, every story, and every fabrication, no matter how big. She did all that she could do to keep people away from her. She had had true love only once, and it had betrayed her. She deserved to be alone for what she was.

She would walk along the edge of the deserts that surrounded the eastern edge of the Village of Inglewood Hamlet. She walked a lot along the grasslands that covered the meadow before the border of the mountains. But it was the deserts that drew her; there was something about the blanched and barren landscape that matched how her heart was feeling. Prudence literally understood the old wives' expression of "love sick", though she had thought this to exist solely in fairy tales and children's stories.

For three years she wandered along the edge of the desert, the grass lush and cool under her feet, the sand calling to her stronger every day. She wanted to wander out into the centre of the sandy plains and never return again.

Late one night, as she sat at the edge of the sands and contemplated her fate, she heard a noise that took her from her reverie.

A man stood in front of her, but he was unlike any man that she had seen before. Even as he stood in front of her, he seemed to be in movement, as if he were made of smoke.

With her heart beating loudly in her chest, Prudence stood and regarded him. Though the robes that covered him were in constant movement, she could see that he was tall and broad shouldered. Dark hair slashed down past his shoulders and framed a pale face that regarded her with concern.

"Are you alright, Prudence Merryweather?"

The being's voice was filled with smoke and floated towards her in the air. If she reached out, she could have touched it. "How do you know my name?"

He smiled. "I know many things…" He reached out and touched a hand to her breast. It was not in a threatening way, but merely a simple gesture of comfort. "I know that you are in pain."

Prudence shook her head, even though tears leaked from her eyes. "I don't know what you're talking about." The words were painful to get out, and hurt to utter.

He shook his head. "You carry so much hurt for the love that was hurting you." He touched his hand to her cheek. His touch was cool and soft, almost like the caress of a cloud. "But you are still breathing, are you not?"

Prudence blinked at him, her eyes wide and glassy. "What do you mean?"

He smiled kindly at her. "Don't they teach you mortals anything of any real importance in your schooling?" He laughed and his smile widened. "Love can hurt you, this is true. Love can maim, destroy, ravage." He took his hand away from her cheek and clasped both of hers in his, though his touch was feather light, as if she were holding smoke.

"But love can also give you joy, glad tidings and feelings that can fill you up with its own kind of magic. But if you're so focused on what was, you will miss what can be." He looked at her with such kindness that it was impossible for Prudence to feel less sad. At his touch, she experienced a sigh that ran through her body and a peacefulness that she had not known in some time.

"What are you?" She asked in a light whisper.

"I am many things," he said. "You can call me Ashe. I am merely smoke and dreams You would call me a spirit, but in our world, I am essentially a Guardian."

"A Guardian for whom?"

"For lost souls." He pointed out into the middle of the desert. "There are those in your village who wonder where the Veil sits? It sits out there, in a place you would perish in."

"Are you death?" She asked.

Ashe shook his head. "No, I am but a guide to those whose time has come. It is not your time Prudence Merryweather."

Tears now leaked down her face in a silent torrent, for no sobs came. Prudence wondered how these could be tears of joy even while she still had such sadness within her. "But I loved him."

"And he loved you. But true love can sometimes burn bright and fast, and flare out just as quickly. It does not mean that there is no more love for you." He wiped the tears from her cheeks, though Prudence did not see how this could be, as Ashe was made of smoke and wind.

"Let go of the hurt, Goodwife Merryweather. When you do, more joy will come to take its place. It does not do to worry of the love that you have lost; instead, love yourself just as much, and the joy will come to you."

Ashe leaned forward and placed a kiss on her forehead. A feeling of such warmth spread through Prudence that she closed her eyes to savour it, to revel in such a feeling of joy. When she opened her eyes, Ashe was gone.

Prudence lived happily from then on. This was not because she had the love of another, but because she had the presence of mind to love herself. She knew that with love, anything was possible.

She knew that, if she loved herself first instead of loving another, everything else would fall into place. Those in the Village of Inglewood Hamlet remarked upon her change, but could only speculate as to the reason for it.

Only Prudence knew the reason for her transformation. She held onto it as if it were a fire. She fed the flame that grew inside of her and knew that it would flare to life again.

So the story goes...

# The Wise Words of a Wind Woman

In the hills of the small village of Inglewood Hamlet, there lived a Wise Woman. The Kingdom of Inglewood resided on the countryside of the Inglewood Township, which was home to Inglewood Hamlet.

On the South Border were the forests, thick and large like ivy dipped in thorns, on the North, her mountains. Who knew what really lay beyond the borders of Inglewood. No one dared venture any further.

Only she had gone the farthest. Most in the village thought that she was insane. She knew this without a doubt. She could see it in their eyes as she made her way across Main Street to the small village that was nestled in the valley, when she needed supplies she could not grow or make for herself.

Who, they whispered, but a wise woman would choose to live in a cave like a Neanderthal? It had always made her smile. She would watch from her perch in the mountains and see them scuttling about their business. This high up, they looked like ants to her, little things that flitted from here to there with no purpose.

She knew that they whispered about her. She could hear their words on the wind. It carried them towards her. Some wondered how she could be so wise, and seem to know everything she did. All they had to do was listen to the wind. This is all she did; people could actually learn a lot if they only bothered to listen.

Just as the wind carried words to her, it carried other sounds equally well. There was the soft crunch of gravel and dirt. Someone was coming up her path.

She already knew who it was. Without turning, the Wise Woman spoke. "I wondered when I'd be seeing you, Goodwife Merryweather."

The crunch of gravel stopped. "How did you know it was me, Wise Woman?"

"I sensed you," she said. "And I could also smell your perfume. No one else wears that particular blend of lilac and lavender blossoms."

"Oh."

She turned with a smile. "You were expecting something a little bit more…mysterious?"

Prudence Merryweather blushed. "I'm sorry, Wise One."

She sighed. "Can we drop all the Wise One talk? I am not one that cares for titles and adornments of unnecessary words."

Prudence's blush deepened further. "Then what should I call you?"

"My name is Gabriella Melissa Montgommery Isise," she said, "But you can just call me Ella."

Her eyes widened. "You're Gabriella Isise?" Her voice was filled with shock. "But she's believed to be dead."

"Ah, but there is not always truth to be found in myths. There are lessons, yes, but not always truth." She smiled and held out a hand to Prudence. "I am indeed alive and well, as you can see."

"But then why haven't you announced your presence? No one in town knew who you were!"

"And why would they?" Ella smiled and gave Prudence a wink. "No one's bothered to come up here and talk to me before."

"But I'm here." Prudence said.

The Wise Woman smiled at her. "Yes, you are." She gestured to a wooden bench that she had carved and waited for Prudence to sit down before sitting beside her. The bench looked out at the forest, her forest really.

As she looked at the trees, the leaves rustled as if they were being brushed with wind. The sight sent a feeling of warmth through her, even now.

"You already know part of my story, then." Ella said. "You know how Gabriella Isise married the love of her life and how he left her, how she came out into the forests and took her own life from grief."

"But then that part of the story isn't true," Prudence said thoughtfully.

"Of course it's not, as I'm sitting right beside you." Ella took Prudence's hand. "You want to know about love. I can smell Ashe and the wind on you. You've been marked by grief."

She uncurled Prudence's hand and traced the life lines that were etched onto the Goodwife's palm. "But there are no marks here," she said. "We are not defined by our scars, no matter how deeply we carry them - unless we let them."

There was a silence that was broken only by the rustle of her trees as Prudence took in the Wise Woman's words. "Why are you telling me this?" She whispered.

"You are marked by loss now, just as I was. I wandered away from my home, far away from it, miles and oceans away from what I knew. My grief filled me so full that it literally poured out of me."

She raised her arm and swept it out to encompass the whole of all they could see. "As I made my way across these plains, then covered with coarse and brittle earth where nothing could grow, I found myself at these mountains."

Ella reached down and grabbed a handful of the earth at their feet. The earth was pebbled with rock and shiny quartz. "There was something here that called to me. I took refuge in them at first, wandering around the insides of the mountains, unaware of the world around me."

She let the handful of earth slip through her fingers, and the two women watched as the wind caught the fragments and slipped them into the air.

"I do not know how long I was inside the mountains. I could not tell you. My grief was so much that time had ceased to matter. But eventually I came to a realisation." She turned back to look at Prudence. "Do you want to know what that revelation was?"

"What?"

"I wasn't dead."

Prudence blinked at the older woman. "That doesn't seem like much of a revelation," the goodwife said.

"Think about it," Ella said. "I thought that my life was over. My heart was broken and I thought my very existence had come to an untimely finish. But I did not die. Indeed, I grew stronger with every day. Eventually I learned that love can hurt, but if it is taken away, it need not be the end." She reached out and took Prudence's hands in hers. "It is only a beginning waiting to happen."

She turned to look again at the valley below them. "When I emerged into the open air once more, I received the shock of my life. For every tear that I had shed, every drop of grief that had over poured from my eyes, a tree had grown. As there are all kinds of different love, there were all kinds of different trees. I walked amongst them and they seemed to know me."

When she turned to look at Prudence again, the woman was regarding her with wide eyes. "Are you saying that you created the forest?" She whispered.

Ella smiled. "Don't you see? They came from my grief. For even from pain there can be beauty. Even from a broken heart, there can be moments of joy. It is all a cycle. It merely depends on how long it takes the heart to mend."

Prudence took her hands back and put them to her breast. "It still hurts, sometimes. Even though I am happy and content with my life, it still hurts."

"That which brings great joy also brings great pain. But you mustn't focus on the negative in life. Your heart is merely aching for another, just as all of our hearts do. You must just remember to embrace that love when it comes and do not turn away from it."

They were silent once more and for a few moments the women listened to the song of the Wind as it sang for them, the rustle of the leaves adding a soft whisper.

After some time, Prudence could not hold back. She had been burning to ask a question. "Did you ever find love again?" She asked. "Did you ever find someone for yourself to match the ache in your heart?"

Ella's eyes were not sad or filled with grief when she turned to face her. "No, I've only had one love in my life." Her smile deepened. "But I am alright with this. I have my trees, the wind that comforts me, the earth that grounds me." She held out her hand to the valley again. "For me, this is enough. There are some that only find one love in their life, some have many. It all depends on how much the heart can want or stand. Each person is different."

She placed a hand against Prudence's cheek in comfort and looked deeply into her eyes. "But I see so much more love for you, Goodwife Merryweather. You need not worry so."

Prudence relaxed into the comfort that the Wise Woman gave her. Finally though, she opened her eyes and asked the other question that she had wanted to put voice to.

"Just how old are you?"

Ella let out a laugh that sounded like water over rocks melded to the softest of birdsongs. "Oh, there are some secrets that the heart must keep, don't you agree?" She asked, giving Prudence another wink.

The two women laughed together at that. Those in the Village of Inglewood Hamlet that heard the song of laughter on the wind that afternoon experienced a most particular emotion of joy.

It filled them with warmth and kindness towards one another. It reminded those that ached from a broken heart of the better things in life. It reminded those that had lost a loved one, and those that had befallen hard times, that good times were coming.

But the thing that most of the villagers wondered about was not the feeling of joy they all experienced, but the gorgeous song that followed it, as if love had been given a voice and been released into the branches of trees blooming with flowers.

So the story goes…

# The Scribe's Wish

In the Village of Inglewood Hamlet, there was a young Scribe who wanted to believe in what he wrote, but despaired that this would never be so.

There were many strange wonders in the Village of Inglewood Hamlet. The villages whispered about the disappearance of the Royal Family, the appearance of an angel, and the shape of smoke that flitted around the borders of the desert. Yet nothing drew their attention quite like the forest.

The Kingdom of Inglewood resided on the countryside of the Inglewood Township, which was home to Inglewood Hamlet. On South Border were the forests, thick and large, like ivy dipped in thorns. On the North were the mountains, matched in height only by the Castle that regarded the town like a giant chess piece, its shadow growing and changing with the heat of the sun.

The Scribe would often wander the forests, though many in the village thought he was risking his own safety to do so. The Scribe knew the old legends; he knew that the villagers whispered that the forest was created by magic, that a Goddess walked amongst the earth and it was her tears that created the trees, the water that roamed along the south end; that from her pain, there came beauty.

Though he wouldn't admit it, the Scribe was looking for something magical. He spent his time scratching away with his quill and papyrus paper, writing down the stories that he carried within him, desperate to be out in the world, ink on paper that would make them somehow more real.

The Scribe knew that he should do something more worthwhile with his education. He was one of the few within the village that knew a trade and many of the villagers thought that he should have taken a job in the town council office, keeping minutes and notations of meetings.

But the Scribe did not do this. He worked deep within the halls of the Inglewood Hamlet Book Room, a sprawling, squat building that housed what passed for a library. During any time of day, the Scribe could be found there, sitting amongst books and papers, their dust rising and falling in the air as if the books were breathing, scratching away with his quill and ink.

Except for when he walked amongst the dark trees of the forest. He did this often, three times a day. He knew that walking amongst these trees only encouraged the whispers of the other villagers, but he paid them no mind. He needed the forest, needed the magic he hoped to find but had thus far been unsuccessful.

Instead, the forest provided a respite from the words that flowed within his head. Though he wrote as much as he possibly could, more words came, more syllables and sounds that linked together to form words and phrases. His head was a cacophony of words and they swam through his mind constantly.

The only thing that provided him sanctuary from himself was the forest and its trees that blocked out the sun, their foliage swaying in a wind that was not there. Though his words flitted through him at every opportunity, as soon as he stepped across the border of the forest and into the embrace of the trees, the words quieted.

Instead of characters and stories and plot lines, the Scribe was instead treated to the sound of crunching leaves underneath his feet, the sounds of birdsong high above him and the whispering sway of the tree branches, almost as if they knew he was there and were welcoming him into their fold.

The truth of it was that the Scribe wrote about what he knew he would never have. He wrote of what he would never find, what he could never have. Though he wrote about love in all of its forms, he knew that he would never feel its soft caress along his skin, the soft rumble of a fire that burned within him as if someone had struck a match or lit a flame inside of his body.

Some called what he wrote fairy tales, no more than the scribbling of life lessons to teach children of the workings of the human heart. But the villagers of Inglewood Hamlet did not know that he was really putting his heart on the page in the hopes that someone would recognize his needs and come to him.

Thus far, this had not happened and he knew only heartache instead of the steady pulse of flame that would grow and flicker as a love grew stronger. Instead of the love he craved, he often wondered if all he would find would be the whisper of the trees in the forest.

They whispered now as he walked into them, the silence of his words almost immediate. He stood there for a moment, savouring the blankness of the page inside of him, listening to the wind moving the leaves of the trees like wind chimes.

Moving deeper into the forest than he had dared go before, the Scribe was astonished to find himself at a clearing that was surrounded by a circle of trees. In the centre of the clearing was a deep pond, its waters a silvery gray. But it was what grew out of the water that caught the Scribe's attention.

A rowan tree grew from the water, higher than he had ever seen, its branches reaching towards the sky as if in greeting. Dotted along its branches he could see the red berries surrounded by five leaves that stretched out like a star, as if the tree had caught falling comets in its embrace.

Not knowing why he was compelled to do so, the Scribe went to the water's edge and sat, looking down at himself in the water's reflection. He saw his dark eyes, the slash of dark eye brows, his dark hair covered shorn to a fine buzz that covered his skull. There was also sadness there; even in the reflection of the water, he could see the deepness of his eyes, pools of want in their own right.

He took a stone from the water's edge and held it in his palm for a moment, holding it within his grasp and making a wish. Though he knew that it was not wise to speak a wish aloud, he did so anyway: "I wish for beauty," he whispered. "I wish for true beauty, as it eludes me."

Throwing the stone in a soft arc, it slipped into the water with nary a splash. He kept his eyes closed, trying to visualize his wish as if it were a living thing. Therefore, he was astounded when a voice spoke to him.

"I am always shocked that mortals wish for what is already in front of their faces." There was humour in the voice. "If only they choose to open their eyes."

The Scribe opened his eyes but saw no one standing there before him. "Who is that?" He asked. "Is there anyone there? Why can't I see you?"

"Just because you can't see me does not mean that I am not here,." the voice spoke again. "I am right in front of you mortal; all you have to do is look."

The Scribe looked in front of him but all he saw was the tree. "There is nothing in front of me."

"You search for beauty, do you not?" The voice asked. It came from all around him, almost as if it were echoing through the branches. "Do you not see beauty in front of you?"

"There is a tree," the Scribe said.

"And are trees not beautiful?"

The Scribe nodded. "They provide shelter, provide the life blood that water brings, that we all depend on. They provide food and wood for keeping warm."

There was a soft chuckle that moved through the air. "I will thank you not to burn pieces of me for warmth, but I can provide you with warmth in other ways, mortal. All you have to do is believe."

"I do believe," the Scribe said.

"Do you?" There was amusement in the voice. "You write of the love you wish to find, but your sadness keeps you from seeing the love that is right in front of you. Do you truly believe?"

Unbeknownst to the Scribe, tears had begun to slide down his face. "I do," he whispered. "Goddess knows that I do."

Three of the Scribes tears slid down his cheek and along his jaw and fell gracefully into the water, one after the other. With his eyes closed, the Scribe did not notice the glow of light that flowed like ink in the water, emanating from his tears. As one, two, and three tears fell, the glow intensified.

Only when the trees above him began to whisper louder than he had ever heard them before did the Scribe open his eyes. He lost his breath when his gaze fell upon the tree. The glow that flowed through the water slipped up the trunk of the tree and along its branches until the entire tree was cloaked in glowing, pulsing light.

The whisper of the tree leaves intensified as the glow increased. The glow of light became so bright that the Scribe had to close his eyes to shield them from its bright, starlight glare. When the whispering of the tree branches stopped, and the press of light was gone, he opened his eyes.

Instead of the rowan tree that had been stretching its branches towards the sky, the Scribe was looking at a man. He was tall and slender, light blond hair reaching way past his shoulders in straight lengths. There was a kind smile on his face, but it was the eyes that the Scribe noticed the most.

They were a deep blue gray, much like the color of the water that had surrounded the tree. The glow that had spread along its branches now emanated from the man's skin. The Scribe knew that this was no ordinary man.

He made his way towards the Scribe across solid ground that had previously been a deep pond. As he moved, so did the glow along his skin, flittering into the air like stars rising up to the heavens. The Scribe stared at him open mouthed but did not feel any fear. Instead, a great calmness was filling him.

"What do they call you Scribe?" He asked.

The Scribe swallowed. Though he wrote so that he could breathe, his words failed him now. Swallowing again, he regarded the man. "Jaymesone Wolfe," the Scribe said. "They call me Jaxon."

The man nodded and came closer. "It is a good strong name for someone that creates stories." He bowed slightly. "You may call me Andrew Goodfellow."

"Is that your true name?"

"I have many names. As do you, if you search inside yourself. Just as you create many stories that fill the pages of your heart, there are many names that we can choose to call ourselves."

"I don't understand what you mean."

"Don't you?" Andrew held out a hand and helped Jaxon to stand. "You create stories with characters that search for love, all named something different. But they are all you, are they not? You put yourself and your hope on the printed page for all others to see, yet you mask your wishes behind false names, hoping no one will guess at what it is that you want."

The Scribe looked at the man and experienced such a feeling of calm that it resonated with comfortable silence within him. "Are you the tree that was standing here before?" He asked.

"I am. I can only take a human form when one who creates beauty frees me from my other form."

"But why a tree?" Jaxon asked.

"It is the Tree of Stories," Andrew said. "We are all bound by it, and every story that has ever been told rests within its branches. There are some who believe that every great story has already been told, but this is not so. There are always more stories for those that wish to create them."

"How is it that I freed you?" The Scribe asked. "I cannot do magic."

"Do you not create stories out of thin air? Do you not create worlds for others to live in, to walk amongst; words that pull at the hearts of others and make them experience emotions that have been long buried underneath their skin?"

Andrew reached out and cupped Jaxon right cheek, his thumb caressing the skin. "That is true magic. What you do is not a curse, it is a blessing. You make the paper bleed with magic, ink marking a surface where nothing existed before. Surely you know this is true?"

More tears slid down the Scribe's cheeks but there were no feelings of remorse. Instead, the tears symbolized a release of something that he had kept locked within himself. "You are very wise," Jaxon said.

"On the contrary, it is you who are the Sage. You remind me of an old friend of mine. His name was Merline and his magic was very great. He created words too, words that would create magic just as you do."

"I do not create magic," the Scribe said.

"But you do. You are able to take the noise of words within you and create true beauty, ever lasting beauty. Only one with such magic within him could have released me from the bonds of my other form."

When Andrew Goodfellow leaned forward and kissed the Scribe, Jaxon let him, feeling as if he had waited for this moment for all of life, as if his existence had been heading towards this very moment.

When their lips met, Jaxon experienced a feeling of peace that ran through him, entwining itself with the newfound peace that rushed through his veins.

Instead of sorrow, the Scribe could only see the beauty in the forest around him, and the beauty of the man who was right in front of him.

"I have been waiting for you," Andrew Goodfellow said. "Thank you for finding me within the forest."

When they kissed again, the light that ran along Goodfellow slipped along the Scribe's skin until they were both encased in a soft, glowing light. As the kiss deepened, the glow of the light increased, highlighting the trees until all of the shadows disappeared.

Those in the Village of Inglewood Hamlet who saw the light that flowed from the forest experienced many different emotions all at once. Some said afterwards that the wife that they had looked at with disdain was once again the beautiful woman they had fallen in love with.

Others who had looked at their children as burdens saw them now as the innocents they were, their faces shining with hope.

As the light floated above the forest and seeped along the sky towards the village, others who viewed the world with discontent could not fail to see the beauty in a branch bending in the wind, or the subtle dance of leaves as they flew through the air.

Some of the villagers of Inglewood Hamlet wondered at the disappearance of the Scribe. Had they looked deep within the forest, where a pond rested inside of a clearing, they would have seen two rowan trees, their branches entwined in an embrace, stretching toward the beauty of the heavens.

So the story goes…

# The Second Sight of Smoke

Once upon a time, in the hills of the small village of Inglewood Hamlet, there lived a man who was neither alive nor dead. He saw too much and felt too little and wondered if he would ever again feel the stings and arrows that could be subjected on the human body.

The Kingdom of Inglewood resided on the countryside of the Inglewood Township, which was home to Inglewood Hamlet. On South Border were the forests, thick and large like ivy dipped in thorns. On the North, the mountains loomed like sentries watching over the town.

In the East and West, Inglewood Hamlet was bracketed by deserts, wide expanses of golden dunes that sat on either side of the village like bookends. The Guide knew every inch of these deserts, every grain of sand. The deserts were his home and his prison.

Were the villagers in Inglewood Hamlet able to see him, they would have whispered gleefully behind their hands, pointed and stared at his form that had no defined shape. They would have wondered how he had come to wander the sands alone, night after night. They would have gossiped about whether he man, or a spirit made of smoke and mirrors.

But the villagers of Inglewood Hamlet could not see him. The only ones that could were those who had the Sight.

And the dead. The dead could always see him.

As a Guide, Ashe was responsible for guiding those who had passed over towards the Veil, where they would meet their final resting place. Though there were those that believed in heaven and hell, Ashe knew that there were no such places. The only heaven that existed could be found on earth in the life that each person made for themselves.

What was beyond the Veil? Ashe couldn't remember. When he chose to think about it, which was seldom, he could remember the sounds of many voices singing all at once and a calm, comforting blackness that was like an eternal slumber.

That was all that he wished to remember. He had been able to return to Inglewood Hamlet due to the sorrow that he still carried with him. It was this sorrow that covered him like a mantle, like a shroud or hair shirt that at once made him wish for the life he had lived, and to deny that it had ever existed.

The life of a Guide was a troubling one. Only those that held onto something from their past could guide the dead to their final resting place. Only those who held onto something from their living lives could remain, even if only in smoke.

The Guide had forgotten how many years he had wandered the Earth, he had ceased to even spare it any thought. Time only mattered to the living, their daily lives separated into seconds, minutes and hours. Time held no meaning for the dead.

He would wander the deserts, letting the sand that flowed there mark his time like a living hourglass, waiting for the souls to come to him. He would see them as they came to the borders of the deserts, transported there by whatever link was forged between the living and the dead. In the daylight, they would shimmer as if filled with water. During the night hours, they would shimmer like candles, their souls burning bright like stars.

It was during the night, the comfort of darkness cloaking him completely within its shadows so that he was all but invisible, that the Guide thought of his sorrow. He thought of it often. The pain he carried in his insubstantial form was a close comfort to him during the nights when the wind howled over the dunes and the skies were bathed in the moon.

He yearned with all of his heart, or what was left of it, to one day see the man he loved again. To one day touch him, though he had no physical body. The touch would be as insubstantial as his form; he knew this, but still he yearned for it.

Tonight was no different. He stood on the tallest dune, the wind whipping sand around him in a dust up, the sand and wind melding together like music, like the sound of his soul that filled up his head when it was quiet. It was a loud and, if he had teeth, they would be chattering in the cold.

In the distance, he saw the shimmering form of a lone soul walking towards him. This was something new to the Guide. Normally, the souls stood on the edge of the desert, wary to step across the border that separated the land of the living from the land of the dead. Normally, he would have to guide the soul gently, approach it with caution. They often did not know that they had died and were about to pass on to whatever awaited them in the afterlife.

Not so with this soul. It burned brighter than any he had ever seen before, and it came towards him with confident steps that failed to make an impression in the sand. Despite being approached so boldly, the Guide stayed where he was. There was something different about this soul, about this shining beacon of light.

That was not the most startling thing, however. Looking down at himself, the Guide saw an answering glow that began to pulse from deep within his own shadowy form. As the light from the soul pulsed, so did the light within him. "What magic is this?" He whispered.

Finally unable to ignore the soul any longer, the Guide drifted down towards him. As he did so, the light pulsed and throbbed within him, stronger in force and intent. When he was fully in front of the soul, he felt his heart stop and his breath leave him. Or, he amended; it would do so if he had either anymore. "Bastien?" The Guide whispered. "Is it really you?"

The soul smiled and the light within him grew brighter beyond recognition. The Guide had never seen anyone, or anything, so beautiful. "I wondered if I would find you here, Maximus."

The Guide moved forward and ran what passed for a hand along Bastien's jaw line, tracing it with what remained of his fingers, though they were only smoke and shadow. "I thought I would never see you again," he whispered.

"And I you." There was pain in these words, pain beyond reckoning. "Have you wandered the sands all this time because of me?"

The Guide stiffened. "This is what I am now." He said. "I am smoke and shadow, nothing more."

Bastien regarded him with sad eyes. "You carry so much pain within you."

"You put it there," Maximus spat out. "What are you doing here anyways?"

Bastien laughed, the sound soft like the rustle of leaves in the sunshine. "Isn't it obvious?" He held out his hands, their brightness leaving tracers in the darkness, to encompass his form. "One can only appear this way when dead."

This softened the Guide momentarily. "How did you die?"

"I don't know if I should tell you."

"Why not?" Despite himself, and the hurt he carried inside of himself, the Guide was curious.

"It will only upset you."

"No more than what you have already done."

Bastien moved towards him, closer than he had been before. So close that the Guide was able to see his smoke body reaching out to entwine himself with the light that poured from the man that he had loved; that he still loved.

"If I could take back time," Bastien said, "I would. I would never have let you leave me; never let you walk out of that door. Do you know how often I wished that I could redo what I did?"

"Never."

"Often," Bastien corrected. "Every single moment of every single day. I had never experienced a love like the one that bloomed between us and it frightened me, terrified me. It was easier to turn away from you than to welcome you into my embrace."

The light inside of the Guide grew with Bastien's words, but the Guide paid it no heed. The sorrow that he kept so tightly locked within himself began to seep into him again, filling him with a delicious melancholy.

"But you did," the Guide said. "You did let me go, rather than face the love that we shared. Do you want to know why I died, how I died?"

Bastien said nothing but nodded his head.

"I died of a broken heart," he said. "My love for you filled every waking moment, every sleepless dream. Soon, it became easier just to rest in slumber, because at least I could be with you in dreams."

Droplets began to fall from Bastien, little beads of light that littered the sand around them. It was a moment before Maximus realized that Bastien was crying. But now that the words were free, he continued, fearful that he would never be able to say them again. "When you told me to leave you, it was as if I left part of my heart behind, part of myself that was still within you."

More droplets fell but Maximus was unaware that they were now falling from his face. The light that had flared to life at the sight of Bastien was now swimming through him, giving his smoky form a shape that it had lost long ago.

"I would drug myself, drink myself to a stupor, all so that I could rest in slumber and be with you. I was consumed with you, enraptured, but you could only bring sadness. One day, I didn't wake up."

"I remember," Bastien said. "I remember when they found your body. My heart ached for you then." He took in a shaky breath. "It beats for you now."

"Don't patronize me," Maximus said. "I don't want to hear your lies."

"But it does. It still beats for you; it pulsed for you even when I stayed away. You asked how I died. Do you want to know?"

Maximus was silent but nodded.

"I died from a broken heart as well, but it was mended at the sight of you."

Maximus let out a derisive laugh. "You expect me to believe this?" The words were filled with the want he felt for Bastien, even now. "How can you expect me to believe that?"

"Can't you feel it?" Bastien asked. "My love for you never died, even if my flesh did. Your heart beats the same way, I know it does. Look at yourself."

Maximus did and experienced the first moment of fear he had felt for some time. For what does a shadow man have to fear? But he was afraid now. His form, normally undefined and fluttery, was now full and bright like Bastien's. As the light in Bastien pulsed, so did the light inside of Maximus.

"What magic is this?" Maximus asked for a second time. He looked at his bright shape with wonder.

"There is no magic," Bastien said. "There is only love."

"I don't understand," Maximum said.

"Love is impossible to understand," Bastien said. "All you have to know is this: even death cannot stop true love. Though bodies will rot away and hearts will stop pumping life blood through veins, love needs no body. Love remains."

There was silence between the two of them and they listened to the whip and snap of the wind and sand. But as they stood there, so close to each other, closer than the Guide had ever let himself get since his heart was shattered, the Guide began to hear a beautiful music.

It sounded as if voices were singing in a harmony that no human voice could ever match. It took only a moment for Maximus to realize that the music was keeping tune to the light that shone inside of them, kept tune with the throb and pulse of the light that made the darkness glow as if they had caught they had drunk down the moon.

"Even now, you still love me," Bastien said. "Tell me this is so."

A sob broke free from Maximus and he uttered only one word. "Yes." He took another deep breath. "I have always loved you. I waited my whole life for you, my whole after life."

With a blinding flash, the light inside of both of them flared to a brightness so bright that, had a mortal been walking along the sand dunes, they would have been blinded. "What magic is this?" Maximum said for a third time.

"There is nothing more pure than love," Bastien said. "There are those that turn away from it when it arrives, when it comes to them, and those that welcome it into their embrace." Bastien moved closer still. "Let me welcome you into mine."

Letting go of the hurt that had given him a form of smoke, Maximus stepped forward and wrapped himself around Bastien, feeling his lover do the same. When the sadness was gone, there was only brightness and the brilliance of love that shone like a beacon to all those who had wished for something more.

In the Village of Inglewood Hamlet, Larry Crockette, the Butcher, remembered a woman that he had loved once and resigned himself to speak to her again. Anastasia Elgine remembered the man she had loved more than any other, and a feeling of beauty slid through her skin, covering her in its warmth. Daphne duMarier turned to her husband, with whom she had been quarrelling, and took his hand, leading him towards their bedroom.

Others in the Village of Inglewood Hamlet saw a light that flared bright and brilliant from the centre of the desert. Some said that it was surely ghosts; some said that it was the work of spirits. Some said that it was the moon falling to the earth, and the brilliance was caused by the sand creating sparks along the moons surface.

Had the villagers been brave enough to venture into the desert, they would have found a small oasis of trees where the light had been. In the centre of these trees, there was a shallow pool that shone like light trapped underneath water, as if it carried the stars in its depths.

If the villagers had been brave enough to step through the trees and look at the surface of the pool, they would have seen two shapes shining like wishes given a body, entwined forever more in an embrace.

So the story goes....

# The Beautiful Sound of Song

Once upon a time, there was a small country by the name of Inglewood Hamlet.

There were four borders to the country, marked by the cliffs, the fields, the sands and the waters. Inside a tower that was located on the very highest point of the cliffs, there lived a Princess named Pam. One day, Pam's life changed forever.

When she thought back on it, Pam decided that out of all the moments from the day her life had changed, she would remember the birdsong most of all. It had been a harbinger of the change she had been so desperately wanted. She had thought she was happy with her lot in life, but that was before she had seen the bird.

Pam had woken early, her handmaiden had brought her breakfast on a little silver tray and she had dressed in one of her most luscious gowns: gold brocade with details in silver. It had no petticoats so it fell to the floor. She loved how it would sweep along the ground, almost as if it were whispering to her while she walked.

She had taken a cup of strong tea made from camomile blossoms and ginger root out into the garden. Her handmaiden, a lovely girl by the name of Anna, would have her breakfast ready upon her return. It was always this way.

Every morning, Pam awoke, dressed, went for her walk with a cup of tea and she would look at the wall, wondering what was beyond it. Then she would return to her tower to break her fast and she would read for the rest of the day. It had always been this way.

Being a Princess was an easy job, but frightfully boring. She spent her days in her tower, surrounded by a wall which was almost as high, with only Anna for company. Anna was a kind soul and good company, but she longed for her Prince. That was the whole point of the Princess gig, after all.

Her job was simple: amuse herself until her Prince came along. That was all well and good, but in her experience (which was albeit very limited) most men needed to be given direction. She had lived in her wall encased tower for forty years. She was now well past the accepted age for a Princess, but she didn't care. She still wore her small tiara, despite the fact that she should be wearing a crown and ruling by now.

The country of Inglewood Hamlet was a small country that did well, even without a ruler. They had had a King and Queen and a Prince before, but they had all disappeared. Pam was the only one left in the royal line to rule and her country didn't need her. So not only was she imprisoned in the tower, when she got free, she would merely be a figurehead, nothing more.

It was as these thoughts ran around inside her head that she herd birdsong. She stopped, looking for it. Though she had trees and a garden inside the walls of her tower, they were too high for most birds. It had been years since she had seen any wildlife. The wall was higher than any bird was willing to fly, higher than any squirrel or chipmunk was willing to climb, so there were no animals in her walled tower garden.

That's why even the sound of birdsong was alarming. She looked around and finally located the bird, a male blue jay. He stood on the edge of the tower wall, serenading her with song. She stood there with her eyes closed, the tea in her hand forgotten, and just listened to the beautiful sound of song.

Her eyes snapped open when the song stopped. The blue jay was still there, but something was happening to him. A light started glowing from his feathers, as if he were made of the sun itself. The glow intensified until he a ball of light, brighter than the sun itself. She shielded her eyes but kept looking. Pam had never seen anything so beautiful.

With a soft pop, the light disappeared, but in its place was a man.

He sat on the edge of the wall, clothed in leather breeches and a poet's shirt, both blue in colour. She put he hand down and lay the teacup on the ground. Pam could only stare at him. He had a strong chin with soft layer of stubble upon it and long dark hair that hung to his shoulders. He had blue eyes that were so clear and so bright, they seemed to be looking right into her.

"Pray, what did you do with the bird, sir?"

"Oh, he's right here. Why don't you come up and fly with me?"

She laughed even as the sound of his voice stirred something in her. "I have no wings. Why don't you come down?"

"Would that I could, dear lady. I would break my legs if I jumped from here and the wall is too tall to fly down into, I would never be able to fly out again. There is a magic that prevents this, shimmering over the top of the tower."

"Fly? You were the bird that sang so sweetly?"

"Yes."

"Then are you a shape shifter?"

He cocked his head to the right as if thinking of how to respond. "Does it matter?"

Pam thought about it for a moment. "No, just sing for me again. It was so beautiful."

"Come up here and I shall. You are the most beautiful woman I've ever seen."

Blushing, Pam asked him: "What do they call you?"

"I am Gregory. I've heard the maiden you live with call you Pamela."

"Pam, please, there's no need for ceremony here. If you've watched us, why are you only showing yourself now?"

"I was afraid, dear lady. There are not many who would have me as I am. I was afraid of showing myself to your maiden."

"Ann would have loved to hear you sing. Are you sure you cannot come down here?"

"No lady, look." He picked up a stone that sat on the walls edge and threw it at the opening at the top of the tower. Something sparked in the sky and it was gone. Then the sky shimmered as if made of water. "It is as I've said, there is a barrier."

"So you mean to tell me that this is the reason no Prince has come to my aid?"

"Why do you need the help of a Prince? You merely have to help yourself to break free of this life and live the life you want."

"How am I to get up there?" Pam asked. "It's so high, you ask the impossible."

"Nothing is impossible if you believe. You have to believe, Pam. Grow wings and come fly with me."

"It's that simple?"

"Yes. You just have to believe."

"There must be more to it than that."

Gregory shook his head. "You are talking to a shape shifter, a being once thought to be mythical yet here I am talking to you. Come on Pam, believe."

The third time he said the word, a breeze came down to run its fingers along Pam's skin and through her hair. She shivered with wanting and closed her eyes, wishing that she could find a way to lift herself up into the air, that she could find a way to sit beside Gregory.

She wished with every fibre of her being but it was not to be. She was saddened that she would not get her happily ever after.

"Pam, open your eyes."

Pam did so, and nearly screamed: she was floating off the ground and a curious light was emanating from her skin. "What magic is this?"

"You're just like me, Pam."

"No, I can't be."

"You're unique and beautiful. Grow your wings. Believe in yourself."

Pam did the only thing she could do: she closed her eyes and did as Gregory told her. She took in a deep breath, taking in the scent of the breeze that had so enticed her. She took in another breath and it was as if her blood had become the air itself.

Her whole body had become lighter. She reached out to touch something, anything, and realized that she didn't have fingers. Opening her eyes, she saw that she had wings. It was as if she was floating on a cloud of light, so bright was the light that emanated from her.

When she reached the top of the wall, she slid through the layer of magic that was there as if it was water. She felt it slide along her skin and then a hand grabbed hers. Gregory looked into her eyes. "I won't let your fall. I won't ever let go of you."

"Nor I. I'm yours for life, if you'll have me."

Gregory pulled her closer to him and Pam's body swooned with need for him. "That's a good thing as blue jays mate for life."

There was a blinding flash of light and a blue jay dance in front of her. It pulled at her hair playfully and sang at her. Pam laughed and let the breeze run through her body until she glowed briefly bright and then transformed.

Pam let out a song of her own. Finally, she knew freedom. She finally knew love. Gregory let out another burst of birdsong and Pam let out her own as she followed him through the air and towards her future.

So the story goes…

# A Scribes Wish Granted

Once upon a time, in the village of Inglewood Hamlet, there lived scribe.

He would tell tales bigger and wider than the impassable sands that bordered the Eastern side of the kingdom. He would spin tales of love that could fill the waters that bordered the Western side of the kingdom. He would write with his quill and paper well into the night, until his candles had burned down to stubs.

Many asked him how he wrote such moving tales of love. Surely there must be an inspiration? He would smile politely and thank them for their compliments, but would say he didn't know where the inspiration came from.

The truth was, he wrote about what he wished for. There were a few times he thought he had found love, but it was of the darker variety. It would start out light and beautiful like a flower come to bloom, but every time it would end the same way, as if it were a flower with thorns that would make him bleed the tighter he held onto it.

So the Scribe let go of the dream of ever finding love, the other half of him. It was simply the way it had to be. He spent his days watching his friends fall in love and build lives with others. He could see the trees that they had planted together taking root in the ground and growing into gorgeous trees full of leaves. They could not see the trees, but he could. It was part of the Scribe's curse, seeing that which others could not see.

When the whispering of the leaves became too much for him, he took himself to the furthest point into the Eastern border, deep into the sands that made up the desert. He built himself a small hut. He didn't need any more space than that; space enough to sleep, eat and write. He lived only for his words now.

On his seventh night in the hut, away from civilization, he received a visitor.

He heard the sound of bells, playing a delightful tune that made him want to get up and dance to their tune. She always arrived this way. He remained sitting and put down his quill. A light began to shine in the middle of his hut and soon, it grew brighter, more vibrant. The light began to hum along with the sound of the bells and, with a small pop, she stood before him.

Her wings didn't have much room to flutter in the small hut, so she kept them close to her back. Looking around at his living quarters, she huffed out a small sigh that sounded like wind flowing through leaves. "Well, I can see why you moved here, Jaxon. This is so spacious and lovely, it just takes my breath away."

Jaxon let out a breath. "Good day, Suzanne. To what do I owe this pleasure?"

"Is that any way to greet your mother?" She smiled and moved closer. "Come give me a hug."
He stood and did so, holding his mother in his arms. She was so much smaller than he was. Though she was Fey and had the smaller stature like all her kind, he knew she possessed the heart of a lion. When he went to pull away, she held on for one last squeeze and his body was filled with light.

Like all Fey, she had magic. Hers was the gift of light and wisdom. Her touch always brought light in the darkness and made your mind clear when it was clouded. To some, this was not a great gift, but Jaxon knew it for the power it was. She had inspired many an artist, helped many law makers in the land make sound decisions and had brought light to people most in need.

Now, she gave him the look he knew so well. "I'm worried about you, Jaxon. Why do you hide yourself away like this? To what purpose?"

"You wouldn't understand."

"Oh, I've lived for hundreds of years and have seen more than you can begin to dream of. Really, why do you live like this? You came from magic and have magic all your own, with words that bring dreams to so many. Why do you hide away as if you are nothing?"

"It's easier that way. I won't get hurt that way."

"You are hurting yourself. Do you not want to find love?"

"I do, but it isn't for me. I've tried."

"Then try again. You have to be open to love for love to find you. When was the last time you went on an outing? Almost a year ago now?"

"Sounds about right."

"You write of the love you wish for, the love you desire, yet you hide yourself away where you cannot possibly meet any man you desire. Is there no one in Inglewood that has shown you some interest?"

Jaxon fiddled with his quill. "Well, there is one man. A man at the money lenders who I've spoken to through letters. His last few missives have become more open and honest."

"Well, if he's shown you interest, than perhaps you need to show some back."

"I wouldn't know where to begin."

"It's quite simple, people have been uttering this magical words for eons now."

"What word is that?"

"Hello. It all begins with hello. The story blooms from there. When do you next go into town?"
"This afternoon. I'm almost out of ink and could use a new quill."

"Fabulous. Then we have time."

"Time for what?"

"To clean you up."

"I look fine."

His mother let out a small laugh. "I mean no disrespect Jaxon, but you look as if you've rolled with the pigs. You smell like it, too."

She waved her hands and the little hut he lived in was filled with light once more. However, this time he was the source of the light. He was filled with warmth and heat and every part of him hummed with magic. When it faded, he looked down at himself.

His ratty trousers were new and made of a thick weave of cotton coloured in grey. His shirt was new too, and made of a finer weave than his trousers. He even wore a little vest that was coloured in shades of gold and silver.

"I don't look like me."

"Yes, you do. You look like everyone else sees you now. Your magic, Jaxon, it's time you started acting like it. Now, did you need a lift to town?"

"No, that's quite all right, I-"

Suzanne snapped her fingers and he was standing in front of the money lenders, quick as a flash. He really hated it when she did that. He had his bag slung over his shoulder, filled with his inkwells. He stood there in front of the money lenders, not sure what to do.

Wanting to gather courage, instead of going in the money lenders, he went to a small pub that served some elixirs and foodstuffs. As his eyes adjusted to the darkness of the pub, he saw a spark of light in front of him.

The man he had been speaking to through letters, Mikhail, was there at a table; and he was looking at him.

It was as if he were propelled forward. With a few steps, he was in front of Mikhail. Though Jaxon had sensed his kindness through his letters, nothing had prepared him for seeing Mikhail in the flesh. Jaxon's heart beat with something he could not name at first, so foreign it seemed within him. However, after a few moments, he could put a name to that emotion: Hope.

He smiled at Mikhail and said the only word that came to mind: "Hello."

"Hello." Mikhail responded

As Jaxon looked into Mikhail's blue and grey eyes, the hope within him grew brighter. The light inside of him matched the light that shone from Mikhal's eyes, and that light came from inside of him.

There are those that said on that day in the small village of Inglewood Hamlet, the sky was filled with stars. Others said that surely a great and powerful witch or sorcerer had cast a spell so large it could be seen miles away. Even more said that they saw a bright light emanating from the pub that filled them with every happy memory they had ever experienced.

There was one woman who knew what had happened, however. She looked out from the clouds at the light shining below and knew that the light meant that her son had fallen in love, so pure and powerful was the light.

So the story goes...

# A Scribes Heart Completed

Once upon a time, in the village of Inglewood Hamlet, there lived a Scribe and his lover.

The Scribe wrote stories of love that were so real to so many people in the village and the surrounding townships, many villagers felt that the characters were people they knew or friends that they had known for a long time.

Oddly enough, Jaxon knew his characters better than he knew most people. They were all a part of him. They were wiser than him, more adept at speaking their mind and following their hearts. He wished that it was just as easy for him to do so.

When he met Mikhail, the money lender had enthralled him Jaxon his kindness and his strength of spirit. Jaxon had never met anyone like him. Mikhail was chivalrous, funny, and incredibly smart and so down to Earth that Jaxon wondered if was made from the Earth itself.

They were out one morning, in the pub they had met in, having coffee when it happened. Jaxon realized he was in love with Mikhail. It was as if someone had lit a candle inside of him, so warm was the love he was carrying inside of him.

Jaxon almost dropped his coffee cup when there was a throb in his heart. He realized it was his heart starting again after being still for so long. He must have let out a small noise, for Mikhail took his free hand.

"Are you all right? Is there anything that pains you?"

Flushed with desire for Mikhail, Jaxon shook his head. "No, I'm all right. Just a little light headed."

When he looked into Mikhail's eyes, their blue-grey colour seemed to be even brighter than it had been only a second ago. Sparks jumped from his fingers and Jaxon wondered if it was because of the candle inside of him.

When Mikhail noticed the sparks, he only smiled. "This is new. You really are magical."

Jaxon blushed an even deeper red and more sparks jumped out of his fingers. "Oh, this happens when I haven't written in a little while." He said. He wasn't sure he could tell Mikhail what had caused the sparks. It was too soon, he had only known Mikhail for a month or so. It was too soon.

"Let me take you home then so you can write. One must not ignore their passions."

Jaxon's heart warmed even further at his words and even more sparks escaped his fingers. Despite the sparks, Mikhail took Jaxon's hand anyway as he took him home. The sparks didn't bother him, even though Jaxon was afraid they would hurt him.

Far from being afraid of the strange changes taking place inside of Jaxon, Mikhail only held on tighter to his hand. The candle flame within Jaxon grew brighter still and more sparkles fell from his fingers.

"I'm sorry, I don't know what's causing this." He said. He couldn't tell Mikhail the truth, that he was completely in love with him. Jaxon was so worried about doing anything that would make Mikhail run.

For his part, Mikhail only brought Jaxon's hand up to his lips and kissed it. "You have nothing to apologize for. Simply be yourself. You're a scribe and that's a certain kind of magic, isn't it?" Mikhail kissed him softly on the lips. "Never apologize for being you. I'll see you later this evening, yes?"

Jaxon assured him that he would and stepped inside his small living quarters. Unlike the tent he lived in previously, this new bedsit had walls and a proper floor, places for his books and a desk to write upon. It was a virtual palace to him after spending so long in the desert sands.

Trying to calm himself, Jaxon went to his desk, drew out his new quill and a bottle of ink and took out some parchment. He was writing. He was penning a tale of two men who had come together to find each other, despite life trying to keep them apart.

He wrote for an hour, feverishly filling up page after page of parchment, that he did not notice his bed sit was now filled with sparkles and the pages themselves now let out their own sparks. He was so intent on what he was writing that he didn't even notice the wind that had started building inside his small nest of rooms.

Jaxon knew none of this of course, so intent was he on his writing. He only noticed when a particularly strong blast of wind came from the pages he was writing on. He was blown back onto the floor as the pages whirled around him. He shook his head to clear it and was startled to hear another voice in the room with him.

"So sorry about that. Let me help you up."

A hand reached down to take Jaxon's and pulled him up onto his feet. Jaxon was astounded to look into the face of one of his hero's, a man named Gabriel. Jaxon would know his light hair, blue eyes and chiseled features anywhere.

"How can this be? How are you here inside my bedsit?"

"Well, don't you know? Look around you."

It was then that Jaxon noticed the brightness inside of his home. The sparks and sparkles filled every corner of his home with a light golden light. Jaxon felt as if he could step onto the clouds of light and walk upon it.

"I don't understand."

Gabriel smiled. "Don't you? The light inside of you for Mikhail is so bright, so alive, that it can't help but escape. It's in your word, in your stories, in you. You write so beautifully of love that you bring your characters to life."

"How do I stop this?"

"Why would you want to?"

"I can't tell Mikhail that I love him, I just can't. He'll run away, I'll frighten him away."
"How do you know that he doesn't feel the same about you? You have only to listen to your heart and let your words do the rest. It you don't let the light out, let it flow, it'll remain trapped, having to find other ways out of you."

"What will happen if I tell him?"

"You'll have to find out. You write your own story. Why do you want to stop it before it's begun? Be honest about how you feel. It's the only way."

Jaxon was about to respond when there was a knock at his door. He turned toward it and then turned back to Gabriel only to find him fading away into a cloud of sparkles that joined the rest of them. Jaxon went to the door and opened it.

There stood Mikhail, surrounded by a shining gold cloud of sparks and sparkles and Jaxon wondered if he had ever wanted anyone more. "Mikhail, I have something to tell you."

"Me first. I have something to tell you." He stepped into the bedsit and took Jaxon into his arms. He kissed Jaxon softly and when he pulled away, he was smiling. "I love you." He said quietly. "I know it's too soon, it's too early, but I can't help that. I feel that I loved you from the moment I first saw you. You are the other half of my heart that I didn't know existed. Please tell me you feel the same way?"

The candle inside of Jaxon reached a fever pitch and he wasn't shocked to see that his skin was glowing. He wasn't surprised to see the same light coming from Mikhail's eyes, the light of his heart shining through for all to see.

"I love you too," Jaxon said. "Beyond all comprehension, beyond words. You complete me." When they kissed, the light inside of both of them flowed out of them and reached far into the sky. Everyone who saw the light was changed that day.

Ladies who had long pined for other men and woman in the village found them and professed their love. Older people remembered the love they had long ago and instead of being filled with sadness were filled joy. Sailors returned to shore to find their wives and husbands and tell them how much they loved them. Men who had long gone without love realized they already loved someone and went to find them so that they did not lose their chance at love and happiness.

When Jaxon broke the kiss, his bedsit was filled with thousands of little sparks and sparkles that pulsed with light in time to the beating of their hearts. "See?" Mikhail said. "You're magical."
They kissed again and Jaxon could hear the flutter of the pages upon his desk as if Gabriel was giving his approval.

So the story goes...

# Afterword

I have always loved fairy tales.

To me, they are the literary equivalent of magic. As a child, I gobbled up Hans Christian Anderson and The Brothers Grimm. There is something in fairy tales that is at once wonderful and thrilling.

The idea I had in the beginning was writing a collection of adult fairy tales about all kinds of love. Each of the stories in this collection focus on a different kind of love: gay, straight, transgendered, inter-racial, long distance love and love even after death.

There is always a lesson to be learned in fairy tales. But, more than that, they delve into the darkness of the human heart and spirit, and force the hero or heroine to confront the darkness that rests inside of them before they can have their happily ever after.

Like the love that inspired the stories, the stories themselves bloomed as I wrote them. I didn't plot any of them and often surprised myself throughout the writing of them.

I had no intention to set a collection of stories in one particular location and thusly, the particulars of Inglewood Hamlet change and shift, like love itself.

While the stories in this collection play loosely with fairy tale traditions, they do hold truths of all sorts within their words. Love is the greatest magic of all. So it's my hope that with all the stories collected, their magic is tenfold.

Whatever you take away from them, I hope you've enjoyed them.

Jamieson

# About the Author

Jamieson has been writing since a young age when he realized he could be writing instead of paying attention in school. Since then, he has created many worlds in which to live his fantasies and live out his dreams.

He is an award winning, Number One Best Selling author of over sixty books.

He currently lives in Ottawa, Ontario Canada with his cat, Tula who is fearless.

Learn more about Jamieson at
www.jamiesonwolf.com